FRIENDS OF ACPL

P9-DDC-007

j
Christiansen, C. B.
A Snowman on Sycamore Street

DO NOT REMOVE
CARDS FROM POCKET

12/96

ALLEN COUNTY PUBLIC LIBRARY
FORT WAYNE, INDIANA 46802

TECUMSEH BRANCH

You may return this book to any agency, branch,
or bookmobile of the Allen County Public Library.

DEMCO

A SNOWMAN on SYCAMORE STREET

A Snowman on Sycamore Street

by C. B. Christiansen

illustrations by Melissa Sweet

ATHENEUM BOOKS FOR YOUNG READERS

Allen County Public Library
900 Webster Street
PO Box 2270
Fort Wayne, IN 46801-2270

Atheneum Books for Young Readers
An imprint of Simon & Schuster Children's Publishing Division
1230 Avenue of the Americas
New York, New York 10020

Text copyright © 1996 by C. B. Christiansen
Illustrations copyright © 1996 by Melissa Sweet

All rights reserved including the right of reproduction in whole or in part in any form.

Book design by Michael Nelson

The text of this book is set in Baskerville BT.
The illustrations are rendered in watercolor.

Printed in the United States of America
First Edition

10 9 8 7 6 5 4 3 2 1

Library of Congress Cataloging-in-Publication Data
Christiansen, C. B.
Snowman on Sycamore Street / by C. B. Christiansen ; illustrated by Melissa Sweet.
p.   cm.
Summary: Angel, Chloe, and Rupert build a snowman and spend the winter
helping one another and playing together.
ISBN 0-689-31927-4
[1. Snowman—Fiction. 2. Winter—Fiction. 3. Friendship—Fiction.]
I. Sweet, Melissa, ill. II. Title.
PZ7.C45285Sq   1996
[Fic]—dc20
95-43883

For Barbi Gronewald Papenfuse, pal
—C. B. C.

For my friend Debbie
—M. S.

Contents

1

The Snowman

Snowflakes fell on Sycamore Street.

Angel and Chloe and Rupert Raguso built a snowman.

"Brrr," said Angel. "He needs a scarf. I'll borrow my mother's scarf."

Angel and Chloe and Rupert Raguso found Angel's mother's silk scarf. They brought it outside.

"It's pretty," said Rupert.

"It's brand new, too," said Angel. She wrapped the scarf around the snowman.

"Brrr," said Chloe. "His head looks cold. I'll borrow my daddy's hat."

Angel and Chloe and Rupert Raguso ran to Chloe's house. They came back with Chloe's daddy's hat.

"It's his favorite," said Chloe. She set the hat on the snowman's head. She pressed it flat so it would fit better.

Now the snowman had a hat and scarf, two chestnut eyes, a radish nose, and arms made of cherry tree branches.

"Brrr, his feet look cold," said Rupert Raguso.

"Silly," said Angel. "He doesn't have feet."

"But if he did, they'd be cold," said Rupert. "I'll borrow my grandfather's rubber boots. He always wears them on snowy days."

Rupert Raguso brought out his grandfather's boots. He put them where the snowman's feet would be.

"I'll fill the boots with snow," said Rupert, "so they won't tip over."

Angel and Chloe and Rupert Raguso stood back to admire their work.

"He sure is big," said Rupert. "He's the biggest snowman on Sycamore Street."

"Silly," said Angel. "He's the *only* snowman on Sycamore Street."

"I'm NOT SILLY!" Rupert packed a snowball and threw it at Angel.

"You missed!" shouted Angel. "Silly!" She packed a snowball and threw it at Rupert. It hit with a thud.

Then Angel and Chloe and Rupert Raguso chased each other around the snowman. Snowballs flew. Melting snow seeped under their coats.

"Ahhhh!" screamed Rupert.

"Eeeeek!" shrieked Angel.

"Oooooh!" squealed Chloe.

Round and round they ran, screaming and shrieking and squealing.

Angel's mother came out on her front porch.

Chloe's mommy and daddy came out on their front porch.

Rupert's grandfather came out on his front porch.

"What is going on?" they asked. They looked at the snowman.

Angel's mother saw her soggy scarf. "It's ruined," she said.

Chloe's daddy saw his flattened hat. "It's ruined," he said.

Rupert's grandfather saw his rubber boots, all filled up with snow. "Aha!" he said. "So *there* they are."

"Uh-oh," said Angel.

"Uh-oh," said Chloe.

"Yipers," said Rupert. "Time to go home."

Angel and Chloe and Rupert Raguso took away Angel's mother's scarf and Chloe's father's hat and Rupert's grandfather's boots. Then they said good-bye to the biggest snowman on Sycamore Street.

"Brrr," said Rupert.

"Brrr," said Chloe.

"Brrr," said Angel. "Aren't you freezing, Snowman?"

"He can't answer," said Rupert.

"Why not?" asked Angel.

"Silly," said Rupert. "He's too *cold* to talk!"

2

Rupert's Turn

A cold wind blew on Sycamore Street.

Rupert was sad. His grandmother was in the hospital. She was coming home soon, but Rupert missed her *now*.

He stood in front of the snowman with his hands in his pockets. "Are you lonely?" Rupert asked.

The snowman didn't answer.

Angel came out of her house with a pair of ice skates.

Chloe came out of her house with a sled.

"What are you doing, Rupert?" they asked.

"I'm keeping the snowman company. Doesn't he look lonely?"

Chloe shook her head.

"He looks cold," said Angel.

"How can we warm him up?" asked Rupert.

"We can't use my mother's scarf," said Angel.

"We can't use my daddy's hat," said Chloe.

"We can't use my grandfather's boots," said Rupert. "Maybe we could build him a great big fire."

"He'd melt," said Chloe.

Angel rolled her eyes and started to call Rupert "silly." "Ssss," she said. Then she looked at Rupert with his hands in his pockets. "Sssad," she said instead. "Maybe the snowman is sad."

Chloe looked at Rupert. She nodded. "Let's try to cheer him up."

"Cheer up, Snowman," said Angel. She made a funny face.

3 1833 029/4 2506

"Cheer up, Snowman," said Chloe. She turned a lopsided cartwheel.

"Cheer up, Snowman," said Rupert. He sighed a big sigh.

"I know," said Chloe. "Let's pretend the snowman can talk."

"I'm too cold to talk," said Angel in a squeaky snowman voice.

"I'm so cold my words froze," squeaked
Chloe. "You have to toast them in the toaster to
know what I am saying."

Angel and Chloe giggled.

Rupert shook his head.

"Your turn, Rupert," said Angel.

Rupert frowned for a moment. Then he
said, "I'm so cold my eyeballs have turned into
ice cubes."

"Yuck," said Angel. She stared at the snowman's face.

"Yuck," said Chloe. She turned her head away.

Rupert's mouth twitched.

"I'm so cold my ears froze and fell right off," said Rupert.

"Ick," said Angel. "Where are they now?"

"Ick," said Chloe. She checked the bottom of her boots.

Rupert grinned.

"I'm so cold, you could put sticks in my fingers and sell them from the popsicle truck," he shouted.

Angel and Chloe covered their faces with their hands. "Yewwww," they cried together.

Rupert laughed out loud.

Angel peeked at Chloe from behind her mittens. "I think the Snowman is feeling better," she said.

Chloe peeked at Angel from behind her mittens. "I do, too," she said.

"He doesn't look lonely and he doesn't look sad," said Rupert. "He almost looks happy."

Rupert patted the snowman on the chest. "You *should* be happy," he said. "You're lucky to have friends like us."

3

Noses are Red, Chloe is Blue

Angel and Chloe and Rupert Raguso were making Valentine cards. Chloe cut out pink hearts and pasted white lace on hers. Angel painted hers lavender. Rupert Raguso taped animal pictures onto notebook paper.

"Whew," said Chloe. "Making Valentines is warm work."

"Is not," said Rupert.

"Is too," said Chloe.

"I can't wait for Valentine's Day," said Angel. "My mother is making sugar cookies with pink sprinkles on top."

"I can't wait for Valentine's Day," said Rupert. "My grandfather buys my grandmother a big box of candy. She always shares it with me."

"I just like making Valentines," said Chloe. "Roses are red. Violets are blue. Giving Valentines is my favorite thing to do."

"You made a poem!" said Rupert. He clapped his hands.

Chloe took a bow. She swallowed twice. Then she coughed.

"Noses are red. Chloe is blue," said Rupert. "You're getting a cold."

"Am not."

"Are too."

"Am not!" Chloe sneezed. She couldn't get a cold. Tomorrow was Valentine's Day.

19

The next morning, Chloe woke up with a stuffy nose and warm cheeks and a sore throat.

"You have a fever," said Daddy. "You'll have to stay inside today."

"What about my Valentines?" asked Chloe.

"I'll mail them, sweetheart," said Daddy. He brought Chloe her fuzzy bear and a brand new red plastic headband.

"Happy Valentine's Day," Daddy said as he closed the door behind him.

Chloe frowned. She could see Sycamore Street from her bedroom window. She saw the mail carrier. "His pouch is full of Valentines," she told Bear.

She saw Angel's mother with a bag of groceries. "Those are for making cookies," she told Bear.

She saw Rupert Raguso walking to Angel's house. He carried a gold box. "Everyone is having Valentine's Day but me," she told Bear. Chloe sniffed. She closed her eyes and fell asleep.

Ding-dong. The doorbell rang. Chloe heard voices on the front porch. She heard footsteps on the stairs. She heard knocking at her bedroom door.

"Cub id," she said through her stuffy nose.

"Happy Valentine's Day," said Angel. She handed Chloe a plate of sugar cookies with pink sprinkles on top. She gave Chloe a lavender card that said, "Be mine."

"Happy Valentine's Day," said Rupert. He handed Chloe two candies from his grandmother's gold box. They were the chewy kind Chloe liked best. Rupert gave Chloe a picture of a giraffe taped onto notebook paper. "I long for you," it said.

"Daddy mailed my Valentines," said Chloe, "so I don't have anything to give you."

Angel coughed. "That's okay. You're sick."

Rupert wiped his nose on his sleeve. "Right, you're sick. Why don't you just tell us a poem?"

Angel and Rupert sat on the edge of Chloe's bed. Their cheeks looked warm. Their eyes looked itchy.

Chloe took a deep breath. "Roses are red. Violets are blue. I think I gave my cold to you."

"Did not," said Rupert.

"Did too," said Chloe.

And they all sneezed at once.

"Achoo. ACHOO!"

4

Angel's Angry Day

Two weeks after Valentine's Day, Chloe and Rupert waited in Angel's kitchen.

"Finish your breakfast, Angel," said Angel's mother. "You need a hot breakfast on a cold, snowy morning."

"I hate oatmeal," said Angel.

"You love oatmeal," said Angel's mother.

"Not today," said Angel. "Today I hate this brown sugar. Today I hate these raisins. And today I especially hate oatmeal."

"You got up on the wrong side of the bed," said Angel's mother.

"Really?" said Chloe. "I didn't know there was a wrong side."

"Me neither," said Rupert.

"Don't look so worried," said Angel's mother. "It's just a saying. It means Angel is having an angry day."

"Does that mean no sledding?" asked Rupert.

"I hate sledding," said Angel. "I hate my itchy mittens. I hate the cold weather. And I especially hate pulling my sled up the hill."

"She's grouchy," whispered Chloe to Rupert Raguso.

"She's grumpy," Rupert whispered back.

Angel glared at them both.

"Here's a snack," said Angel's mother. She handed Angel a paper bag with Angel's name written on it. Chloe and Rupert had bags with their names on them, too.

They put their bags in their pockets and their boots on their feet and *clump-clumped* out the back door.

"Have fun," said Angel's mother.

"I hate having fun," said Angel. She slammed the door behind her.

Angel and Chloe and Rupert Raguso pulled their sleds to the top of the hill. They stopped to rest.

Rupert looked into the paper bag with his name on it. "Num," he said. "I have chocolate chip cookies."

Chloe looked into the paper bag with her name on it. "Yummy," she said. "I have peanut butter cookies."

Angel looked into the paper bag with her name on it. "Oh, no!" she said. "Oatmeal cookies." She dumped the cookies in the snow. "I hate oatmeal!"

Three squirrels ran down from a tree and carried the cookies away.

"Aren't they cute?" said Chloe. "I love squirrels."

"Squirrels-*shmerls*," grumbled Angel. "Let's sled."

Chloe went first. "Wheee!" she sang.

Rupert went second. "Yahoo!" he shouted.

Angel went third. "Oooph!" she grunted as she fell off her sled. She rolled and rolled. When she stood up, she was covered with snow.

Chloe laughed. "You look like our snowman!"

Rupert laughed. "Our big, fat snowman!"

Angel wasn't laughing. "It's not funny," she said. "I hate snow! I hate sledding! And I especially hate looking like a big, fat snowman!"

Chloe whispered to Rupert.

Rupert whispered to Chloe.

"Let's go," they said.

"Where do you think *you're* going?" said Angel. She followed behind them, kicking at the snow.

Chloe and Rupert pulled their sleds to Angel's house. They went into Angel's room and pushed her bed against the wall.

"Now you won't get up on the wrong side," said Chloe.

Angel nodded slowly. "Good," she said. "I hate being grumpy. I hate being grouchy and I especially hate an angry day."

"Angry-*shmangry*," said Rupert. And they all laughed. Especially Angel.

5

Snowfriends

The last snow fell on Sycamore Street.

Angel and Chloe and Rupert Raguso came out on their front porches.

Rupert wore new mittens from his grandmother.

Chloe wore her red plastic headband under her hat.

Angel carried a bag of oatmeal cookies.

Rupert was not sad.

Chloe was not sick.

Angel was not angry.

"Let's play!" they shouted to each other.

All morning long, Angel and Chloe and Rupert Raguso rode their sleds down the hill.

At lunchtime they drank hot cocoa with marshmallows.

In the afternoon, they skated on the pond by Angel's house.

"Brrr," said Rupert at the end of the day. "Time to go home. I'm as cold as a snowman."

"Oh, no!" said Chloe. "I forgot about our snowman."

"Me, too," said Angel. "There he is, all by himself."

"Yup," said Rupert. "He's still the biggest snowman on Sycamore Street."

"He's still the *only* snowman on Sycamore Street," said Angel.

"With no one to keep him company," added Chloe.

Rupert shivered. "Then let's make some friends for him."

Angel and Chloe and Rupert Raguso each scooped up a handful of snow. They rolled the snow into great big balls. They stacked the balls next to the snowman—three on one side and three on the other.

Chloe made arms out of cherry tree branches.

Angel made eyes out of chestnuts.

Rupert ran home to get two radish noses.

When the noses were in place, Angel and
Chloe and Rupert Raguso stood back to
admire their work.

"Friends!" said Rupert.

"Snowfriends!" said Chloe.

"Are you happy now, Snowman?" asked Angel.

"Silly," said Rupert. "He can't answer."

"Why not?" asked Angel. "Is he still too cold to talk?"

"No," said Rupert. "He doesn't have lips. How can he talk without lips?"

Chloe took off her red plastic headband and put it where the snowman's mouth should be.

"He's smiling!" said Rupert.

"He's happy!" said Angel.

"Shh," said Chloe. "I think I hear him talking."

"Really?" asked Rupert.

Angel and Chloe giggled.

"I'm hungry," said Angel in a squeaky snowman voice.

"Give me a cookie, please," said Chloe in a squeaky snowman voice.

"Give one to Rupert, too," squeaked Rupert from behind his new mittens.

"Everybody gets one," said Angel. "Rupert and Chloe, Snowman and Snowfriends, and even one for me."

Chloe bit into her oatmeal cookie. "Yummy," she said.

Rupert bit into his oatmeal cookie. "Num," he said.

Angel bit into her oatmeal cookie. "Mmmm," she said in a squeaky snowman voice. "Friends are delicious."